CRUCIBLE OF THE VAMPIRE

A GRAPHIC NOVEL BY
IAIN ROSS-McNAMEE

Adapted from the feature film written by
IAIN ROSS-McNAMEE   JOHN WOLSKEL   DARREN LAKE

Cover design and additional images by
CHARLIE ADLARD

Isabelle's Diary & Scarlet's Letter written by
AMANDA MURRAY

Tourist map painted by
FELICIA DUTTON

1st Edition published in 2018 in Great Britain by Ghost Dog Films

A SIGNIFICANT FIND

A
CONFIRMATION
And Difcovery of
WITCH CRAFT

Courteous Reader,

TO the end I might fvt'iific the opinion of fuchaf defire to he further fatiffied concerning the diabolicall art or crying (in, of Witch-craft (if I may fo call it;) For the finue of Witch-craft and the diabolical practice thereof, if omnivm fcelervm atrociffmvm, and in fuch af haue the knowledge of God the greateft Apoftacie from the faith; for they renovnce God and Chrift, and giue themfelues by a couenant to the Deuill the vtter enemy to God and all mankind, for in Devt. 18. 1 o, 1 1 , 12. God gaue command to all the children of Ifrael that none amongft hif fhovld bee fuch. For thofe abominationf n'ere the children of Canaan driuen ovt from before them and vtterly deftroyed and plagued. Af alfo Manaflet, 2 Cron. 33 (which wickedneff of hif waf fo abhorred of God.

By John Stearne, now of Lawshall neere Burie Saint Edmonds in Suffolke, sometimes of Manningtree in Essex. 1648

NO, IT IS NOT TRUE, SIR!

YOU ARE SUMMARILY ACCUSED OF SORCERY, WITCHCRAFT AND **NECROMANCY!**

NO, 'TIS ALL LIES!

HEAR YE? LIKE HIS MASTER BEELZEBUB HE IS A CONSUMMATE LIAR

WHY, EZEKIEL, YOU WILL HAVE TO DO BETTER THAN THAT

WHILST WE WATCHED YOU FROM AMONGST THE TREES...

... I, THE CAPTAIN AND HIS MEN HERE, ALL PLAINLY HEARD YOU CALLING FOR YOUR DAUGHTER, *LYDIA*

AND YET IT IS KNOWN ABROAD, THAT YOUR DAUGHTER IS DEAD THESE PAST NINE MONTHS

FURTHER, SINCE HER PASSING, LYDIA HAS BEEN WITNESSED WALKING HERE IN JACOB'S WOOD. WHAT GREATER PROOF OF SORCERY DOES ANY GOD-FEARING MAN NEED?

"We are all just little souls
carrying about a corpse"

Epictetus

ENGLAND 2017

YOU WANTED TO SEE ME, PROFESSOR EDWARDS?

I CERTAINLY DO. TAKE A LOOK AT THIS, ISABELLE

DO YOU RECOGNIZE IT?

OF COURSE, IT LOOKS LIKE THE STEARNE CAULDRON

SO NAMED BECAUSE IT WAS AMONGST THE EFFECTS OF JOHN STEARNE...

...ASSOCIATE OF MATTHEW HOPKINS, THE SO-CALLED, WITCH FINDER GENERAL. IT'S IN THE CIVIL WAR COLLECTION, BECAUSE THAT WAS THE TIME THEY WERE OPERATING, BUT THE CAULDRON IS ACTUALLY MUCH OLDER, QUITE POSSIBLY CELTIC, PRE-ROMAN PERIOD

ARE THESE PHOTOS FROM WHEN IT WAS DISCOVERED?

YES AND NO. TAKE A CLOSER LOOK

OH MY GOODNESS. THIS ISN'T OUR HALF OF THE CAULDRON IS IT? **IT'S THE MISSING HALF!**

WELL IT MIGHT BE. THAT'S WHAT I WANT YOU TO FIND OUT. THE PHOTOS AND THIS LETTER WERE SENT TO ME BY A CHAP IN SHROPSHIRE...

... ONE KARL SCOTT-MORTON. BIT OF AN ECCENTRIC I THINK. APPARENTLY DOESN'T HAVE A PHONE, ONLY COMMUNICATES BY LETTERS.

ANYWAY, IT SEEMS HE'D BEEN DOING SOME RENOVATION WORK TO HIS STATELY PILE AND DISCOVERED IT BURIED BENEATH THE FLOOR IN HIS CELLAR.

AT LEAST THAT'S WHAT HE SAYS. HE MAY OF COURSE BE AWARE OF OUR HALF OF THE CAULDRON AND KNOCKED UP A FAKE IN THE HOPE OF RAISING SOME FUNDS

DO YOU THINK IT'S GENUINE?

WELL, OF COURSE I'D LIKE TO. THE FACT THAT IT'S STILL PARTIALLY IN THE GROUND SUGGESTS IT MIGHT BE, BUT YOU'VE ONLY GOT TO LOOK AT THE BRITISH MUSEUM'S EXPERIENCE WITH THE RISLEY PARK LANX TO REALISE THERE ARE SOME *AWFUL* CROOKS OUT THERE

AT FACE VALUE THIS CASE HAS SOME STRIKING SIMILARITIES. IT'S VERY MUCH A CASE OF CAVEAT EMPTOR

YES, BUT THE LANX WAS COMPLETELY LOST AND THEN "REDISCOVERED", WE AT LEAST HAVE HALF OF THE CAULDRON ALREADY

INDEED WE DO – WHICH SHOULD GIVE YOU A CONSIDERABLE ADVANTAGE WHEN YOU COME TO LOOK AT MR. SCOTT-MORTON'S HALF

YOU WANT *ME* TO GO??

ABSOLUTELY. YOU'RE AN ASSISTANT CURATOR NOW AND BESIDES, I HAVE TO DEAL WITH SOME TEDIOUS FINANCIALS FOR ONE OF OUR UNIVERSITY BENEFACTORS

O..OK, BUT IT SEEMS ODD TO ME THAT THIS HAS SURFACED IN SHROPSHIRE. AS FAR AS I UNDERSTOOD IT, STEARNE AND HOPKINS WERE ONLY ACTIVE IN THE EAST OF ENGLAND

WE ONLY KNOW WHAT STEARNE WAS DOING UP TO 1648, WHEN HE WROTE HIS BOOK, "A CONFIRMATION AND DISCOVERY OF WITCHCRAFT"

THE CAULDRON MAY RELATE TO SOME LATER, UNDOCUMENTED ADVENTURE. IF GENUINE, THIS MISSING HALF OF THE ARTEFACT MAY GIVE US SOME ANSWERS

ANYWAY, I'VE TAKEN THE LIBERTY OF BOOKING YOU ONTO A TRAIN UP TO SHROPSHIRE TOMORROW. YOU'VE GOT THE REST OF TODAY TO GET READY

EVERYONE KNOWS THE BIG HOUSE.

HMMM

The County's Favourite Magazine Since 1977

LIVING IN SHROPSHIRE

MAGAZINE

Ashwell Hall, The Country Seat of the Scott-Mortons

Usually a very private individual, local landowner Karl Scott-Morton invited Living in Shropshire Magazine in for a look around his remarkable ancestral home, Ashwell Hall. Nestled in the heart of the Shropshire countryside, Ashwell Hall is a hidden 16th century gem, which, Karl's family bought in the early 1800's. "I think my forebears fell in love with the atmosphere the place has, as much as its splendid appearance." Karl mused.

The place is indeed splendid to behold, especially as Karl and his wife Evelyn have undertaken an extensive programme of renovations over the last several decades. "In the 1980's I'd been living away in France, working as a dealer in antiquities. I met my wife during that time and it had always been our plan to come back to the hall at some point. While I was away, I had let the hall out to be used as a private girls school and when the school's tenure came to an unexpected end, we decided to make the move."

Standing in the grand library, Karl continued, "Mind you, it didn't look like this when we returned. The school hadn't been a good tenant and the place was in a terrible state. They'd left in a hurry and there were beds piled in the hallway, desks here in the library and all manner of mess scattered throughout the house."

Current owner of the Hall, Karl Scott-Morton talks to Living in Shropshire Magazine about his family and the Hall's history

"I was in France at the time, so I'm not sure exactly what happened, but it was an unhappy moment in the Hall's history. Apparently two pupils vanished without trace and the ensuing scandal forced the closure of the school."

Indeed foul play was suspected, as the missing girls were reported being seen some days later in nearby Jacob's Wood, walking with a mysterious woman in black. Something Karl is quick to dismiss.

"I'm sure they just ran away", says Karl, "naturally there were rumours. There are local legends about witchcraft and people's imaginations got the better of them. Of course it's all nonsense."

Walking on around the huge house, Karl explains that in order to keep a grip on costs, he set about the mammoth task of renovating the property, by doing most of the repairs himself.

His wife, Evelyn, had been working as a costume designer for a theatre in Paris and she put her skills to good use too, designing and making endless curtains and other soft furnishings.

"Between us we managed to get the place in some kind of order." Recalls Karl. "I started on the roof, as I felt it was most urgent to prevent any water ingress. Naturally with a house of this age and size, there's always something that needs fixing."

Outside there are extensive grounds to look after too. "Most of the land is let to local farmers", explains Karl, "So it pretty much looks after itself", but we have had to employ a gardener to look after the grounds. Trying to do the renovations myself and manage the grounds would have just been too much."

Although it's been an immense amount of work, Karl believes all the effort has been worth it. "We've managed to restore parts of the Hall to some of its former glory and it's been hugely rewarding too. Our daughter, Scarlet, has grown up here and a better place to have one's childhood, would be hard to imagine. She's a trained ballerina and the ballroom is a marvellous place for her to practice in. The grounds are perfect for her horse riding as well."

Karl and Evelyn's daughter, Scarlet (above)

> ## "There's something magical about the place, you'll never be able to leave"
>
> *KARL SCOTT-MORTON*

Looking to the future, the Scott-Mortons plan to remain at the hall. "We all feel very much at home here." Says Karl. "As a family we've been here for nearly two hundred years now and I can't see that changing. There's something magical about the place that keeps us here. It's one of those houses, that once you step foot in it, you'll never be able to leave."

As we walked along the main gallery I asked

A DREAM OF YOU

SCARLET!!

I'M SURE SHE'S AROUND SOMEWHERE. PROBLEM IS, THIS HOUSE IS SO DAMNED *BIG!*

WHY DON'T I SHOW YOU YOUR ROOM, DEAR?

THE HOUSE WAS USED AS A GIRL'S BOARDING SCHOOL UNTIL QUITE A FEW YEARS AGO

WE HAVEN'T QUITE MANAGED TO RESTORE IT BACK ENTIRELY TO IT'S FORMER GLORY AS A COUNTRY HOUSE

HOPEFULLY THAT WILL ALL CHANGE SOON

WELL, THIS IS YOUR ROOM, DEAR.
I'M SURE YOU'LL BE COMFORTABLE

ANYWAY, LET ME SHOW
YOU THE BATHROOM

NOW YOU'LL NEED A TORCH AT NIGHT, I'VE LEFT ONE IN YOUR ROOM

NOT ALL OF THE HOUSE IS WIRED UP YET AND WE HAVEN'T QUITE GOT AROUND TO PUTTING UP THE LIGHTING

THERE'S ALWAYS SOMETHING TO DO ISN'T THERE?

BEEP... BEEP... BEEP...

SORRY, IT HAS NOT BEEN POSSIBLE TO CONNECT YOUR CALL

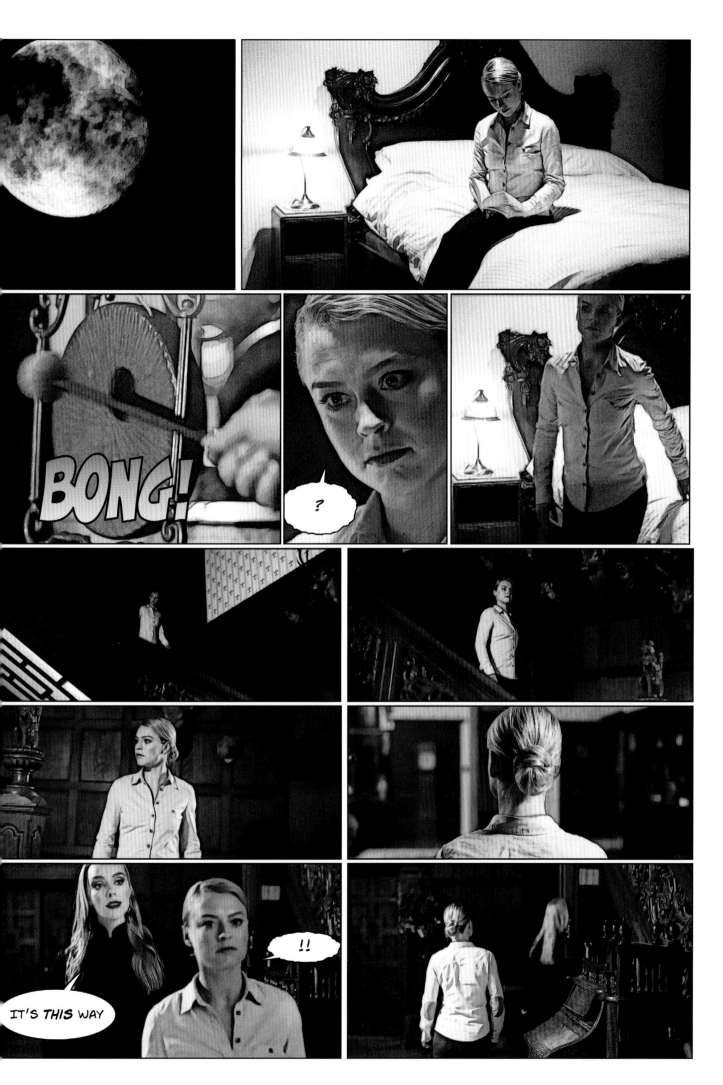

YOU DANCE BEAUTIFULLY

UH, HUH...

SCARLET, WAS THAT YOU WALKING ABOUT LAST NIGHT?

WALKING ABOUT? ARE YOU IMAGINING THINGS?

I THOUGHT I SAW...

LAST NIGHT I WAS SLEEPING PEACEFULLY AND NOW I AM *TRYING* TO DANCE PEACEFULLY

SORRY...

BUT YOU DO... YOU DANCE BEAUTIFULLY

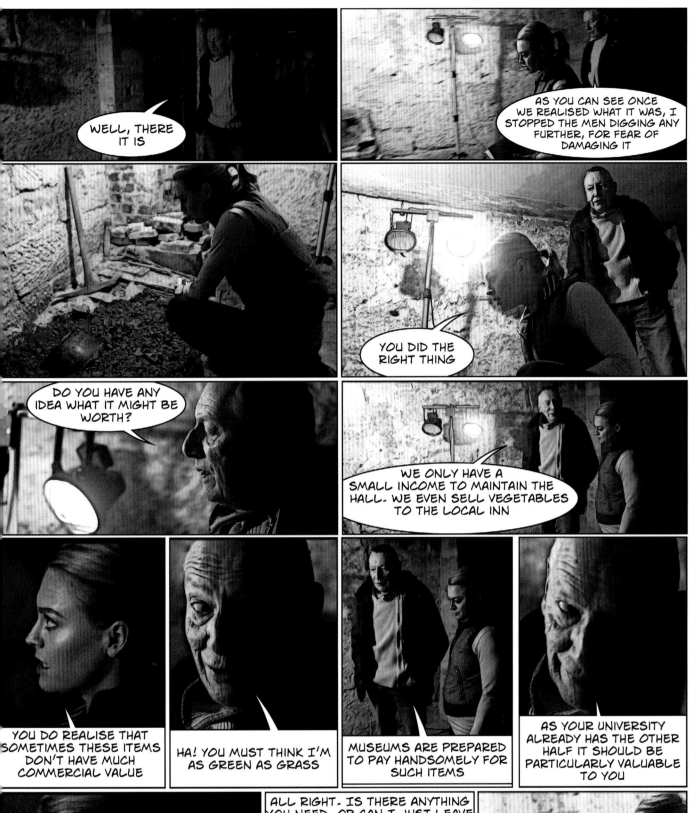

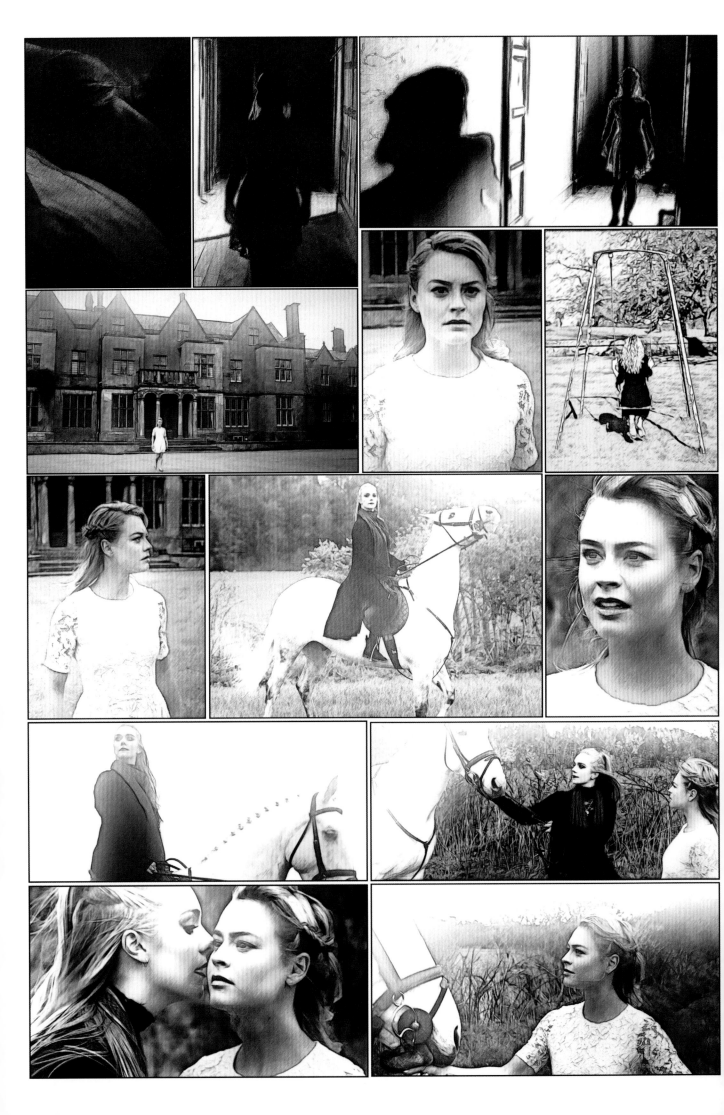

THE CONFESSIONS OF SAINT AUGUSTINE

Wednesday

Tonight I heard a strange clanking noise in the hall and I crept out of my bedroom to see what was happening. As I leaned over the bannisters I could see Karl talking to two men. One of them looked very similar to the creepy taxi driver who drove me here from the train station. It was quite dark and I could barely make out his features in the shadows, but I'm pretty sure it was him. They were also carrying what looked like an old oxyacetylene welding rig. I wonder what they're doing with that? It seems a bit odd to be using that so late at night. Mind you, nothing should surprise me in this place, everyone seems a bit strange!

This gloomy house is full of shadows that play tricks on my mind. I feel like I'm seeing ghosts half the time...

Thursday

Last night Evelyn brought me a hot drink when I was in bed. It certainly helped me sleep, but what strange, vivid, muddled dreams I had. I dreamt I was walking towards the old rusted swing that's under the oak tree on the front lawn. I could see a figure on the swing, dressed in black with light blonde hair. I tried to speak to her but no sound came out of my mouth. As I walked nearer I reached out my hand to the strange figure who sat limply on the swing, her arms hanging at her sides.

I heard the sounds of a horse and suddenly I was in open countryside. I could just detect the fields in the moonlight and my bare feet brushed against the cool grass. Out of the shadows Scarlet came towards me, she was riding a white horse. A beautiful powerful white horse, with its mane plaited and braided. Scarlet looked commanding and impressive, a long red scarf like a river of blood, flowed from her neck down to her thigh.

In the stillness of the night I could hear the sound of the horses hooves thud on the ground and its breath like a ghostly whisper. As I looked up, I saw Scarlet standing in front of me holding the reins. We stood face to face for a while, the full moon between us. She reached out a marble white hand and offered me the reins before melting away. Suddenly I was alone with the white horse.

I was watching her dancing in the ballroom yesterday. She dances beautifully, I wish I could move like that. But she's arrogant and dismissive and we're unlikely to be friends. ~~~~~~~~~~~~~~~~~~~~~~~

SO, WHAT DOES YOUR BOYFRIEND THINK OF YOUR INTEREST IN ALL THIS?

I DON'T HAVE ONE

I DID BUT WE NEVER REALLY TALKED ABOUT THIS STUFF

OH, TO BE LIKE YOU – YOUNG AGAIN. WELL, YOU CAN TAKE YOUR PICK...

"I CAME TO CARTHAGE...

...WHERE A WHOLE FRYING PAN FULL OF ABOMINABLE LOVES CRACKED ABOUT ME ON EVERY SIDE. I WAS NOT IN LOVE YET, YET I LONGED TO BE IN LOVE...

...I WAS LOOKING FOR SOMETHING TO LOVE, I WAS IN LOVE WITH LOVE ITSELF"

HAVE YOU READ SAINT AUGUSTINE'S CONFESSIONS?

NO, I CAN'T SAY I HAVE

YOU REALLY MUST. THERE'S A COPY IN THE LIBRARY. FEEL FREE TO POP IN THERE AND HELP YOURSELF

THIS IS INTERESTING...

THERE IS AN ORIGINAL INSCRIPTION ON THE SIDE OF THE CAULDRON, BUT SOMEONE APPEARS TO HAVE SCRATCHED IT OUT

YES, WELL, I WILL LEAVE YOU TO IT!

AM I RIGHT IN THINKING, YOU'RE ISABELLE, THE ONE DOING WORK UP AT THE HALL?

YES THAT'S RIGHT. HOW DID YOU KNOW?

OH, I'M PSYCHIC. FAMOUS FOR IT ROUND HERE

OH, REALLY?

ABSOLUTELY! IT'S A GIFT...

...THAT COMES FROM WORKING IN A PUB, WHERE EVERYONE TALKS ABOUT WHAT THEY'RE DOING AND SOMEHOW, I KNOW WHAT'S GOING ON!

AH, I SEE. WHO TOLD YOU?

ROBERT, THE GARDENER

THAT MAKES SENSE. I DIDN'T THINK IT WOULD BE MR SCOTT-MORTON

NO, HE'S NOT THE PUB-GOING TYPE. WE HARDLY EVER SEE HIM IN HERE

DO YOU WANT THESE IN THE BACK, VERONICA?

THANKS, ROBERT

SO HOW LONG ARE YOU HERE FOR?

SHAME. NICE TO HAVE A FRESH FACE AROUND HERE

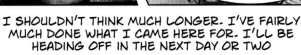

I SHOULDN'T THINK MUCH LONGER. I'VE FAIRLY MUCH DONE WHAT I CAME HERE FOR. I'LL BE HEADING OFF IN THE NEXT DAY OR TWO

SO, WHAT WE TALKING ABOUT THEN?

NOTHING, ISABELLE WAS JUST SAYING SHE'LL BE LEAVING IN A DAY OR TWO

SO WHAT EXACTLY IS IT YOU'RE DOING UP AT THE HALL?

I'D LOVE TO TELL YOU, BUT I'M NOT SURE MR. SCOTT-MORTON WOULD APPRECIATE IT

FAIR ENOUGH. HOW'S SCARLET?

SHE'S FINE. YOU KNOW HER THEN?

YEAH, SHE'S THE ONLY ONE OF THE SCOTT-MORTONS WHO EVER CAME IN HERE... AT LEAST WHEN SHE WAS WITH HER BOYFRIEND... AND SINCE THEY SPLIT UP WE HARDLY EVER SEE HER... HOW ABOUT YOU? BOYFRIEND?

NO, NOT ANYMORE

OH, SOUNDS OMINOUS. DO I SENSE A STORY THERE?

THERE IS, BUT IT'S NOT VERY EXCITING... IT'S A BIT SILLY REALLY

WELL, YOU DON'T HAVE TO TELL ME ABOUT THAT EITHER IF YOU DON'T WANT TO, BUT TRUST ME, WORKING IN THIS JOB, I'VE HEARD IT ALL BEFORE

WELL, IT'S NOT LIKE IT'S A BIG SECRET OR ANYTHING. I HAD A STRICT CATHOLIC UPBRINGING AND I KNOW IT'S NOT THE WAY THESE DAYS, BUT I'VE ALWAYS BEEN OF THE BELIEF SEX SHOULD BE RESERVED FOR MARRIAGE. ANYWAY, RICHARD – HE'S MY EX, JUST COULDN'T COPE WITH THAT

I SEE

AT FIRST HE WENT ALONG WITH IT, BUT AS TIME WENT BY, HE FOUND IT MORE AND MORE DIFFICULT, UNTIL IN THE END IT ALL CAME DOWN TO ULTIMATUMS AND NEITHER OF US COULD COMPROMISE

WELL IT WAS PROBABLY FOR THE BEST. I ADMIRE YOU FOR STICKING TO YOUR GUNS. THE WORLD WOULD BE A LOT SIMPLER IF MORE PEOPLE DID THAT

PROFANUM

Friday

Today's been another strange day! I came across a room I'd not seen before. I'd been on my way back to the cellar to continue my work on the cauldron. I think the Scott-Mortons must have been out, as the house was very still and quiet, so me being me, I couldn't resist the opportunity to investigate.

I think it must be Evelyn's dressmaking room as the place was stuffed with fabrics, mannequins and sewing paraphernalia. Over the fireplace the mantel was covered in beautiful drawings and sketches, similar to the ones that are hanging on the wall in my bedroom. Evelyn told me on the day I arrived, that she used to be a theatre costume designer. I could see that she was extremely talented and could definitely imagine her in that role. She dresses stylishly, even now, and there's something captivating about her French accent. Scarlet's obviously inherited a sense of drama from her mother!

But the room had a really weird vibe. I got a bit freaked out as I thought I saw one of the mannequins moving. It was probably just a gust of air, this place is full of draughts and shadows. And then I found a hooded robe and a mask on a rail of clothes. It's probably something to do with some play Evelyn or Scarlet are involved in. It's all made me feel a bit uneasy though.

"Having retired from a scholarly life in Oxford to the County of Salop, my custom of an afternoon, was to take the airs and walk abroad, familiarizing myself with my new surroundings. On one such excursion, I found myself on the fringes of *Jacob's Wood*, a particularly wild and ancient place, grown all the more so, because local men fear to venture there."

"I have ascertained this is because there are some persistent rumours of witchcraft, which have led to this wood being shunned by all. In this Age of Reason, such beliefs seemed to me ridiculous."

"As I walked along the tangled fringe of the wood, I fancied I heard curious music, faintly drifting on the wind. Intrigued, I stopped and listened."

"The thin, piping, melody seemed to be emanating from the dark bowers of the wood and being aware of the local reputation, my curiosity was pricked. I determined to find its source."

"I struck out into the wood, which having been left abandoned and uncoppiced for many years, was dense and overgrown."

"My progress was slow and laboured, but as I picked my way through the dark bowers of the wood, I could catch the strange, eldritch melody on the breeze."

"Eventually, I came upon a small clearing and as I stepped into it, the melody was no more. Just the sound of the wind in the trees remained."

"As I turned to leave, my foot struck an object protruding from the earth. I would not have remarked upon it, but for it made a singular, metallic sound."

"Clearing away leaves and other detritus I soon concluded I had stumbled upon something quite striking. I toiled to free the item from the earth, which held it in a vice-like grip."

"Having only my bare hands and sticks, such as I could find, it took me some time to lever the item free. It was nothing less than part of a cauldron."

"Returning to the house with my trophy, I set about scraping the soil and grime of centuries from it. The item was bronze and of ancient origin, covered with Brythonic writings."

"Over the next few weeks I set about translating them as far as I was able. The cauldron was no household cooking pot, but a religious item, used in a ceremony of rebirth."

"The story revealed by the antiquated text, was that of a dread queen, slain in battle, who was placed in the cauldron along with the blood of her enemies."

"Through its magical power, she rose again. The name of this queen is lost, as at a later date, someone had been at pains to grind her name and likeness from the cauldron."

"In an act of further vandalism, the Latin word *"profanum"* or *"unholy"* had been etched into the sides of the vessel."

"Other words too, but as they crossed onto the missing portion, I was unable to decipher them. At the time, I took this to be the work of some dull mechanical, afraid of his own shadow, but as the days passed, I too began to fear."

"At first I was plagued by restless, fevered nights and in that chimerical space between sleeping and waking I often fancied I could hear that same melody as I had heard in Jacob's Wood, floating through the house."

"Several times I rose from my bed and searched the house in an effort to locate its source, always without success, until, on one such night, I left my bed chamber and walked the long gallery."

"In the swimming, grainy darkness, a thousand fanciful fiends danced in my fevered imagination. I stopped, determined to put such thoughts from my mind."

"It was at that point, the figure of a deathly pale woman appeared in front of me. I stared at her bleached, cavern-eyed face, etched with a hunger deeper than just a need for mere sustenance."

"Then, in an instant she was **gone**."

"By morning I was convinced my encounter with the awful woman was the product of a fevered mind and attempted to put it from my thoughts…"

"...but several days later I was at the piano and without realising it, I found myself playing the eldritch melody I first heard floating on the wind in the woods."

"As I looked up from the keys I saw her again. So startled was I, that I knocked the key lid down upon my hand and cried out."

"When I looked up the apparition was gone."

"I know that I can no longer stay in this house.

I am resolved to depart forth with."

"I leave this account of the occurrences here, along with musical notation of the melody that accompanies the spectre, as warning to those who come after me."

"God save us all!"
Jeremiah Caine, April 6th 1807.

BANG!

DO YOU THINK THAT WAS FUNNY?

HAVE YOU BEEN HAVING NIGHTMARES? BAD DREAMS ARE COMMON IN THIS HOUSE

I THOUGHT I SAW SOMEONE IN MY ROOM...

WHY DON'T YOU GET INTO MY BED?

YOU COULD SLEEP WITH ME IF YOU WANTED...

HAVE YOU BEEN SEEING SHADOWS IN YOUR ROOM?

THE BEST THING TO HELP YOU SLEEP IS TO LISTEN TO A NICE, SCARY GHOST STORY

THERE WERE LOTS OF HIDDEN PLACES, JUST LIKE HERE

SHE WAS AN INQUISITIVE GIRL WHO WANTED TO KNOW THINGS. CLEVER, JUST LIKE YOU, ISABELLE...

I THINK SHE EVEN LOOKED A LITTLE BIT LIKE YOU

SHE WAS ALL ALONE IN THE BIG HOUSE, TRAPPED LIKE A BIRD IN A CAGE

SHE LAY IN BED FEELING SCARED, BECAUSE THERE WAS NOBODY OUT THERE...

SHE HEARD NOISES TOO, AND ONE NIGHT SHE DECIDED TO LOOK, BECAUSE SHE WAS BRAVE...

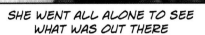

SHE WENT ALL ALONE TO SEE WHAT WAS OUT THERE

SOMETHING **EVIL** THAT HATED THE GIRL

IT WATCHED HER AS SHE LOOKED AROUND ALL ALONE

IT COULD SEE HER...

BUT SHE COULDN'T SEE **IT**...

ISN'T THAT **SCARY**, ISABELLE?

IMAGINE THAT – WALKING ALL ON YOUR OWN IN THE DARK WITH SOMEONE BEHIND YOU BUT YOU DIDN'T KNOW THEY WERE THERE...

READY TO **JUMP** ON YOU AT ANY MOMENT

YOU COULDN'T DO ANYTHING ABOUT IT... IF IT WANTED YOU IT COULD JUST TAKE YOU

ALL OVER YOU, THAT **OVERPOWERING** EVIL...

Footsteps In The Dark

PLEASANT ONES?

A BIT MIXED TO BE HONEST

OH, DO TELL US ABOUT THEM!

WELL, IT'S ALL A BIT OF A JUMBLE

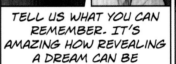

DING DONG

I'LL GO

TELL US WHAT YOU CAN REMEMBER. IT'S AMAZING HOW REVEALING A DREAM CAN BE

UM... WELL, I'M NOT SURE I CAN REMEMBER ANYTHING...

...AS I SAY, IT'S ALL A BIT OF A JUMBLE

OH, THAT'S A SHAME

WELL, NEVER MIND, PERHAPS YOU'LL HAVE THE SAME DREAM AGAIN

IT'S HERE, IT'S HERE. THE OTHER HALF OF THE CAULDRON IS HERE!

COME ON, YOU CAN GET ON AND VERIFY OUR HALF NOW

HUH, SOUNDS LIKE NONSENSE TO ME

WELL, OF COURSE IT IS. BUT IT TIES IN WITH JOHN STEARNE AND ALSO A DOCUMENT FROM THE 1800'S THAT I FOUND IN YOUR LIBRARY. I MEANT TO MENTION IT TO YOU EARLIER...

...IT'S A JOURNAL ENTRY BY SOMEONE WHO STAYED AT THE HOUSE. IT SEEMS THEY WERE FRIGHTENED OFF BY A GHOST. YOU KNOW I SAID I HAD A DREAM AT BREAKFAST...

THERE ARE NO GHOSTS IN THIS HOUSE. I WOULD KNOW...

LOOK, SHOULDN'T YOU BE CALLING THE PROFESSOR TO TELL HIM THE NEWS

OF COURSE I WILL, BUT I NEED TO FINISH...

...A FULL EXAMINATION OF THE CAULDRON, SO I CAN BRIEF HIM PROPERLY, THEN HE CAN GIVE YOU A MORE ACCURATE IDEA OF THE VALUE. IT'S GETTING LATE NOW, I'LL DO IT IN THE MORNING

WELL, YOU'D BETTER BE UP BRIGHT AND EARLY THEN, HADN'T YOU?

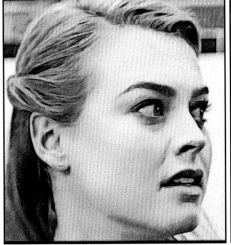

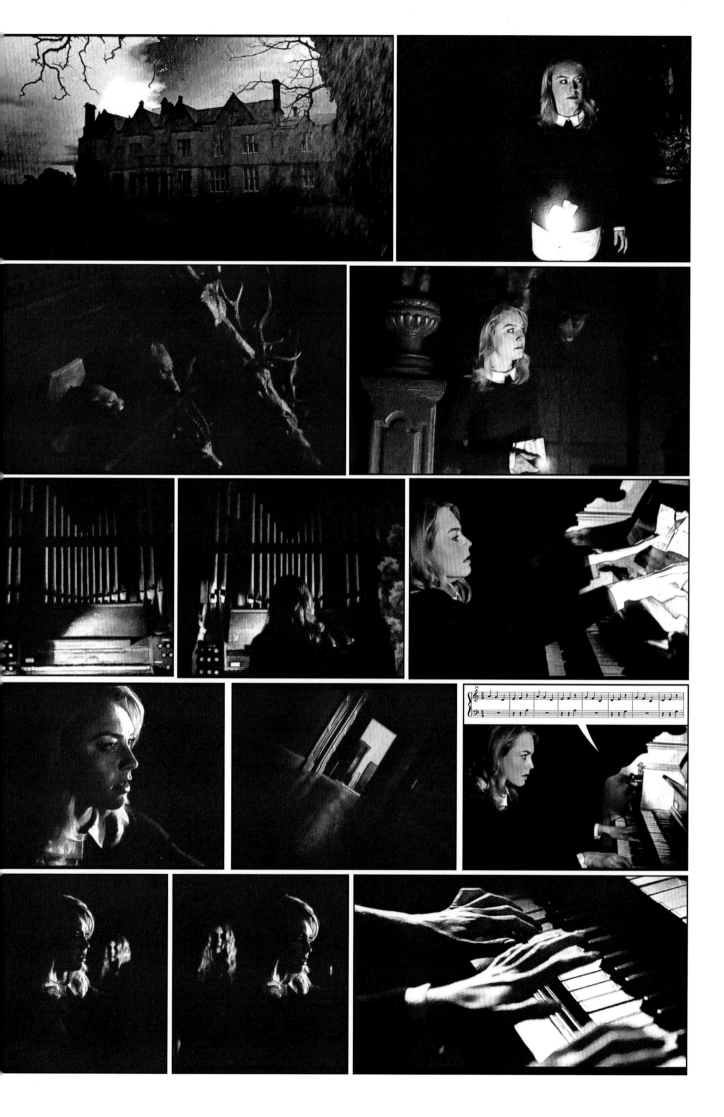

THE CRUCIBLE

My Darling,

It's past midnight and I've been lying here in the dark for hours, thinking of you and trying to find the right words to tell you that I can never see you again.

Our time together was so precious and I have so many memories that I'll always treasure, but I'm sorry, it's all over.

Please don't ask me why, you just have to trust me and believe me when I say that our relationship has run its course and has to end.

I know there'll be dark days ahead for both of us but life goes on and you will soon forget and move on even though I know the pain and loss sometimes feels endless.

I've destroyed all your letters and ask that you return mine to me. Part of me will always love you, but please do not contact me again,

SCARLET

ISABELLE!

I WAS WONDERING IF YOU COULD GIVE ME AN OPINION ON SOMETHING I'VE BEEN MAKING...

...IF YOU HAVE A MOMENT?

WOULD YOU LIKE SOME REFRESHMENT?

I'VE BEEN WORKING ON A WARM PRESSÉ

I KNOW YOU THINK YOU SAW SOMETHING LAST NIGHT

YOU SEEM QUITE JITTERY ABOUT IT

THIS DRINK WILL SETTLE THOSE NERVES

IT'S A COMBINATION... APPLES, OPIATE HONEY, CAMPHOR, EXOTIC SYRUP... BLACK SEEDS...

HAHAHA, I CAN GIVE YOU THE RECIPE, IF YOU'D LIKE

I... I SAW HER. YOU'RE HIDING SOMETHING!

CRASH!

UGGG...

WE ARE ALL JUST LITTLE SOULS CARRYING ABOUT A CORPSE

....

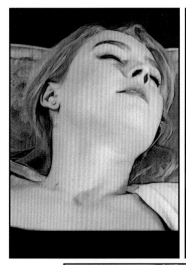
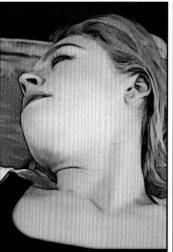
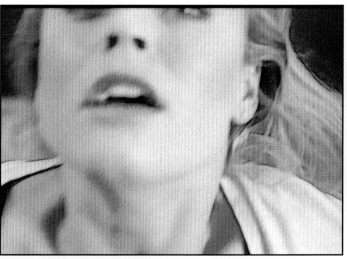

AHHH!

KARL, PLEASE. LET ME OUT OF HERE. LET ME GO. I WON'T SAY ANYTHING. I JUST CAN'T BE TIED UP, PLEASE!

OH NO, THAT'S NOT GOING TO HAPPEN. YOU'RE STAYING HERE. I'M AFRAID YOU KNOW TOO MUCH

KNOW TOO MUCH? YOU MEAN THAT GIRL I'VE SEEN?

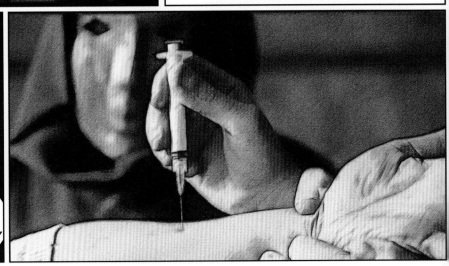

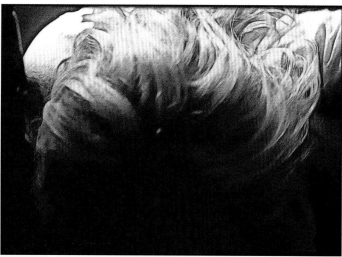

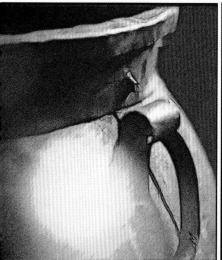

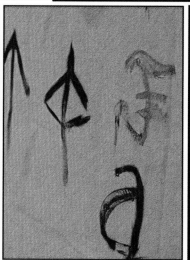

CRASH!

EEEEIIUUU!!

THWACK!

NOOOO!!

AAAAHHHH!!

CRACK!

UUUGGHH!

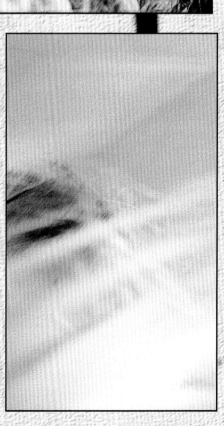

FOOTSTEPS

AAAAHHHHHHH!!!!!!

AAAAHHHHHHH!!!!!!

CLICK!

AAAHHHHH!!!!
!!

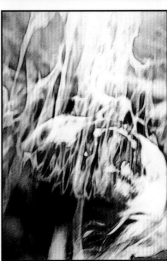

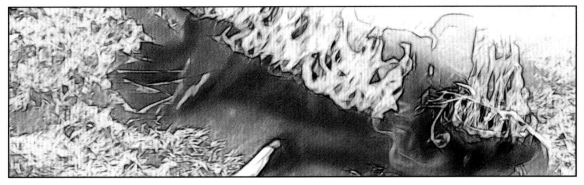

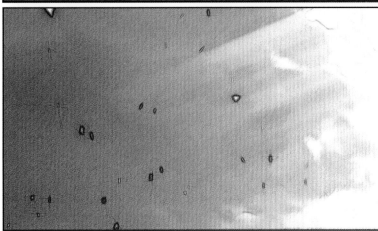

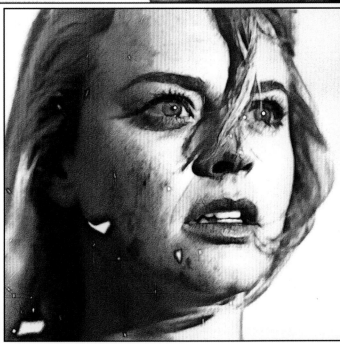

ADAPTED FROM THE FEATURE FILM

CRUCIBLE OF THE VAMPIRE

Starring

Katie Goldfinch - Isabelle

Florence Cady - Scarlet

Neil Morrissey - Robert

Larry Rew - Karl

Babette Barat - Evelyn

Lisa Martin - Lydia

Aaron Jeffcoate - Tom

Brian Croucher - Ezekiel

Charles O'Neill - Jeremiah

Angela Carter - Veronica

Richard Oliver - Taxi Driver

John Stirling - Stearne

Phil Hemming - Professor Edwards

Michael Molcher - The Captain

Jeremy Taylor - Soldier

David Rowlinson - Soldier

Peter Rowlinson - Soldier

Graham Langhorne - Soldier

Pete Yeo - Stranger in house

Directed by
Iain Ross-McNamee

Produced by
Amanda Murray

Written by
Iain Ross-McNamee
John Wolskel
Darren Lake

Executive Producers
Howard Thorne
Gordon Howdle

Music by
Michelle Bee

Colourist
Neill Jones

Sound Mixer
Rick Smith

Choreography
Vikki Burns

Makeup
Karolina Kluzniak

Cinematography
Richard Carlton
Iain Ross-McNamee
Ben Davies

Sound Recordist
Len Usselman

Visual Effects
Patryk Enerlich

Horse Trainer
Dean Price

Stunt coordinator
Justin Pearson

Historical Advisors
Dr Georges Kazan
Rev'd Canon William Price

Associate Producers
Richard Bowler
Bruce Crawcour
Bryan Daniel
Christopher Evans
Mark Hinks
Steve McNamee
Ian Norris
Philip Northwood
Diana Packwood
Gerald Rogers
Adam Smith
James Thorne
Pete Wasteney
Rob Wasteney
Philip White